A Doggy Tale
And Two Tales on Top

A DOGGY TALE
AND TWO TALES ON TOP

KAREL ČAPEK – JOSEF ČAPEK

ALBATROS

PRAHA

A DOGGY TALE

For as long as my grandfather, the miller, delivered bread around the villages and brought fine grain back to the mill, everyone knew Fido: well, Fido, anyone would tell you, that's the little dog that sits on the driver's seat beside old Bilker, and looks as though he was driving the whole cart; and if it's a bit slow going up hill, he starts to bark and straight away the wheels turn faster, Bilker cracks his whip, Freddie and Sadie – those were my grandfather's two horses – pulled hard and now the cart was running triumphantly into the village and giving off that lovely scent of God's gift of daily bread. And that, children, is the way Fido, now deceased, rode around the whole parish.

For in his day, you know, there were none of those crazy motorcars; at that time one rode slowly, properly and made oneself heard. No chauffeur in a motorcar knows how to crack a whip as beautifully as the late carter Bilker, god bless him for ever, or to click his tongue at the horses as he did; and no chauffeur has wise Fido sitting beside him, driving the horses, barking and spreading terror – none of that. A car just flies past and leaves a stink behind it, and now look where it's got to, you can't even see it for dust. As I say, Fido drove more thoroughly; for half an hour beforehand

5

people pricked up their ears, sniffed and said: "Aha!" For they knew the bread was on the way, and they came to the threshold to give it "good day". And now Grandad's cart really is running into the village. Bilker clicks his tongue, Fido barks on the driver's seat and suddenly hop! he jumps onto Sadie's rump (and she had some rump, I can tell you, broad as a table it was, four people could have sat down to dinner at it), and now he's dancing along Sadie's back, running from collar to tail, from tail to collar, and it seems as though he must split his jaws for pure joy: bow–wow, boys, bless me, we didn't half speed along, me and Freddie and Sadie. Hurrah! And the boys' eyes almost pop out. The bread comes every day, and always it's such a ceremony, as if the emperor himself were coming! – Well, as I say, nobody has driven for ages as thoroughly as in the days of Fido.

And Fido knew how to bark as if a pistol were going off. Bow! to the right, so the geese ran in fright: ran and never stopped till they got to the green in Fifield, quite amazed at how they got there. Wow! to the left, so the pigeons from the whole village flew up, circled round only to settle beyond St. Weonards, not to say over the Welsh border. So loud could Fido bark, bless his heart, and it was a wonder his tail didn't fly off, the way he wagged it for joy when he made all that noise. Well, he had something to be proud of, there isn't a general with such a loud voice, maybe not even a member of parliament.

And yet there was a time when Fido didn't know how to bark at all, even though he'd outgrown puppyhood and had such fine teeth that he chewed up Grandad's Sunday--go-to-meeting boots. For you should know how Grandad got Fido, or rather how Fido got Grandad. One day Grandad was going home rather late from the pub, and as it was

6

night and as he felt merry, and perhaps even to drive off evil spirits, he sang as he went. Suddenly, in the dark, he lost the right note and had to stop and find it. And as he was searching he heard some sort of whining, whiffling, whimpering sound at his feet; he crossed himself and felt over the ground to find what it could be. He touched a warm, fluffy little ball that fitted into the palm of his hand, soft as velvet it was; and as soon as he held it in his hand, it stopped whimpering and sucked his finger, as if it were made of honey. I must have a look at that, thought Grandad, and he took it home with him to the mill. Grannie, poor dear, was waiting up for Grandad, so she could say good night to him; but before she could phrase it suitably, wily old Grandad said:

"Just look, Nellie dear, what I've brought you." Grannie shone a light on it, and look there now, it was a tiny puppy, just fancy! A doggy baby still blind and yellow as the kernel of a nut. "Well I never," Grandad was surprised, "but Puppy-kins, who do you belong to?" The puppykins, of course, said nothing; it trembled on the table like a bag of misery till its little rat–tail bounced, and it squeaked grievously; and then, just imagine, a little puddle appeared under it and spread like a bad conscience. "Charlie, Charlie," Grannie nodded gravely at Grandad, "have you taken leave of your senses? That little mite's going to die without its mummy." At that Grandad took fright. "Quick, Nellie," he said, "warm up some milk and bring some white bread." Grannie got everything ready. Grandad soaked the soft crumbs in the milk, tied it into the tip of a handkerchief and made such a good teat that the puppy sucked at it till its tummy was tight as a drum.

"Charlie, Charlie," Grannie nodded her head again, "have you taken leave of your senses? Who's going to keep that puppy warm, so it doesn't die of cold?" But you don't know Grandad, he wasn't a man to be opposed! He grabbed the puppy and took it straight to the stable; and on my word, it was lovely and warm in there, heated by Freddie's and Sadie's breath! The two horses were asleep, but when their master came in, they lifted their heads and followed him with their wise, kind eyes. "Freddie, Sadie," said Grandad, "we're not going to harm this Fido in any way, see? I'm putting him under your protection." And he laid the tiny Fido in the straw in front of them. Sadie sniffed at the funny little creature and smelt her master's well-known hands; and she whispered to Freddie: "it's ours!" And that was that.

So Fido grew up in the stable, feeding off the teat of a handkerchief, till his eyes opened and he could drink from a bowl himself. And he was as warm as if he'd been with his mummy, so he soon became a little rascal with a silly head. Well, a puppy doesn't even know where his bottom is to sit on, so he sits on his own head and is surprised it hurts; he doesn't know what to do with his tail, and as he can only count to two, he mixes up his four legs. In the end he flops flat in amazement and lolls out a little tongue that's as prettily pink as a sliver of ham. But anyway, every puppy is like that, in short, like children. Freddie and Sadie could tell you more; they would tell you what a worry it is for an old horse, taking care all the time not to step on a crazy little dog; you know, good people, a hoof is not a bedroom slipper and it has to be stood on very slowly and lightly so that something on the floor doesn't start to squeal in pain and complain. Well, children are a cross we have to bear, Freddie and Sadie would tell you.

And Fido grew into a big dog, happy and toothy like any other dog, yet there was something missing: nobody had ever heard him bark - not even growl. He just made a kind

8

of whistling or wailing noise, but it wasn't barking. And one day Grannie said to herself: How is it that Fido doesn't bark? She thought it over. For three days she went about like a body without a soul, and on the fourth day she said to Grandad: "Why is it that our Fido never barks?" Grandad thought it over, for three days he walked about and kept on shaking his head. On the fourth day he said to Bilker, the carter: "How is it that our Fido never barks?" Bilker took the matter thoroughly to heart; he went to the pub and there he thought for three days and three nights; on the fourth day he was feeling a bit sleepy, somehow his head was a bit muddled, and he called the inn-keeper and pulled some coins out of his pocket to pay what he owed. He counted and counted, but the devil himself must have mixed him all up and he couldn't get it right. "Why Bilker," said the inn--keeper, "didn't your mother ever teach you to count?" At that moment Bilker didn't care what he'd spent, he slapped his forehead and ran to find Grandad. "Master," he shouted from the doorway, "I've got it! Fido doesn't bark because his mother never taught him to!"

"Bless my soul!" said Grandad, "that's true: Fido never knew his mother, Freddie and Sadie never taught him to bark, there's no other dog in the neighbourhood, so Fido doesn't even know what barking is. You know, Bilker," he said, "you'll have to teach him to bark."

So Bilker sat down in the stable with Fido and taught him to bark. "Bow-wow," he explained to him, "notice how it is done; first a vrrrrr here in the throat, and then suddenly you let it out of your mouth: bow-wow. Vrrrr, vrrrr, bow--wow-wow!" Fido pricked up his ears, this was music that he somehow liked, without knowing why; and all at once, for pure joy, he barked. It was rather a funny sort of bark, it screeched like when a knife skids over a plate, but every

beginning is rather hard; after all, you didn't know your alphabet straight away. Freddie and Sadie listened and wondered that old Bilker was barking; but then they shrugged their shoulders, and from then on they never took Bilker seriously. But Fido had an extraordinary talent for barking, he learnt quickly, and when first he went out with the cart it was bow to the left, wow to the right, as if he was shooting from a pistol; in fact till the very end of his life Fido never grew tired of the sound of his own barking and he barked all day long; so happy he was to have learnt it properly.

11

But riding with Bilker and driving was not the only thing Fido had to do. Every evening he would go round the mill and the yard, making sure that everything was in its place, going for the hens, so they didn't cluck like old women at the market, and then he would stand in front of Grandad, wag his tail and look intelligent, as if to say: Just you go off to bed, Charlie, I'll take care of everything, So Grandad patted him and went to bed in the fear of God. But in the daytime Grandad often went around the villages and townships, buying grain and all sorts of other things, maybe clover seed, lentils or poppy–seed; and then Fido ran alongside him, and when they went home at night he wasn't afraid of anything and found the way even if Granddad, himself, sometimes missed it.

So one day Grandad was buying seed somewhere, in fact it was in Munsley; he made his purchase and then stopped off for a moment in the pub. Fido waited in front of the pub; but then something good tickled his nostrils, such an exquisite smell from the kitchen, that he had to go and have a look. And truly, there were people eating sausages; so Fido sat himself down and waited to see if some of those delightful sausage skins didn't fall under the table. And while he was waiting a cart stopped in front of the pub belonging to Grandad's neighbour, what on earth was his name? Maybe Jones; Jones found Grandad in the tap–room, one word led to another, and then the two neighbours ran out to the cart, like they'd go home together. Off they drove and Grandad clean forgot about Fido, while Fido was in the kitchen, sitting up begging for sausages.

When the staff of the pub had finished eating they threw the sausage skins up on the stove to the cat; Fido got short shrift and only then remembered where he'd left Grandad. He searched and sniffed all over the pub, but Grandad was nowhere to be seen. "Fido." said the inn-keeper, "your master drove off out there," and he pointed the way. Fido understood that and set off home alone; at first he went along the road, but then he said to himself: "I'd be silly to do that, I'll take a short cut across the hill." So off he went over the hill and through the wood. It was already evening, then night fell, but Fido wasn't at all scared. Nobody's going to steal anything from me, he thought. But he was as hungry as a dog.

Night had fallen by then, and a full moon came out; when, in places, the trees had stepped back a little in a glade or clearing, the moon appeared over the tree-tops, and it was so beautiful, so silvery, that Fido's heart beat in astonishment. The forest rustled softly as if harps were playing. Now Fido was running through the forest like a dark, black tunnel, but suddenly a silver light shone in front of him, the harps seemed to be playing louder, and every hair on Fido's body stood up on end; he crouched down to the ground and gazed as if bewitched. Before him was a silvery meadow and dancing on it were fairy dogs. They were lovely white dogs, but absolutely white, indeed translucent, and so light on their paws, they didn't even shake the dew from the grass; well, they were fairy dogs, Fido knew that at once, because they lacked that certain interesting little smell by which a dog recognizes a real dog. There was Fido lying in the wet grass with his eyes popping out of his head. The fairies were dancing, chasing each other, wrestling with one another, or running after their own tails, but all so lightly, so airily, that not even a blade of grass moved beneath them. Fido took careful notice: if any of them started to scratch or bite at fleas, then it wasn't a fairy but a white dog. But not one of them scratched or bit at fleas; so that was the holy truth, they were fairies. When the moon

13

was very high the fairies lifted up their heads and began to howl and sing gently and beautifully; not even the orchestra in the National Theatre could do it so well. Fido was so moved that he cried, and he would have sung along with them if he had not been afraid of spoiling everything.

When they had finished singing, they lay down around a very noble old dog, probably a sorceress or powerful fairy, quite silver and delicate. "Tell us a story," begged all the fairies.

The aged dog fairy thought a while and then she said: "I will tell you how the dogs made man. When God had created the whole world and all the animals, he put the dog at their head as the best and the wisest. All the animals in paradise lived and died and were reborn happily and contentedly, only the dogs were sadder and sadder. So God asked the dogs: "Why are you sad when the other animals rejoice?" And the oldest dog said: "You see, God, the other animals lack nothing, but we dogs have got a bit of sense in our heads, and with that sense we realise that something exists that is higher than us, that you exist, oh Creator! We can sniff at and smell everything, only not you, and we dogs miss that very much. Therefore, Lord, fulfil our wish, and create for us a god whom we can smell." And God smiled and said: "Bring me some bones and I will create a god that you can smell." And the dogs ran around and each of them brought a bone: this one a lion's, that one a horse's, one a camel's, another a cat's, briefly bones of all the animals except a dog's; for no dog will touch either dog's meat or a dog's bone. Then there was a big pile of those bones, and from the bones God made man, so that dogs should have their own god whom they could smell. And because man was made of all the animals' bones, except dogs', he has the qualities of all the animals:

14

he has the strength of the lion, the industriousness of the camel, the cunning of the cat and the magnanimity of the horse, only he has not the dogs' fidelity, not the fidelity of the dog at all!"

"Tell us another story," begged the dog fairies again.

The aged dog fairy thought for a while and then she began: "Well then, I'll tell you how dogs came to heaven. You know that peoples's souls go to the stars after death, but there was no star left for dogs' souls, so that after death dogs' souls went to sleep in the earth. That was until the time of Jesus Christ. When people scourged Christ tied to a pillar, a terrible lot of blood was left there. And a hungry stray dog came and licked Christ's blood. "In the name of Mary," exclaimed the angels in heaven, "that dog has received the blood of the Lord!" "If he has received the blood of the Lord," said God, "we shall take his soul to heaven." And he made a new star, and to show it was meant for the souls of dogs, he gave it a tail. And as soon as a dog's soul came to the star it was so fantastically delighted that it started to run and run and run all over heavenly space, like a dog runs about a field, not in an orderly way along the path like other stars. And those dogs' stars that romp about all over heaven and wag their tails are called comets."

"Tell us more," begged the fairy dogs for the third time.

"Well then, I'll tell you," the aged fairy began, "that many, many years ago dogs had a kingdom on earth, and a big dogs' castle. But people envied the dogs their kingdom on earth and they wove spells until, at last, the dogs' kingdom, with the castle, fell into the depths of the earth. But anyone who digs in the right place will burrow down to the cave where the dogs' treasure is still hidden."

"What is the dogs' treasure?" asked the fairies eagerly.

16

"Well," said the aged fairy, "it is a hall of the most splendid beauty. The columns are made of the loveliest bones, but not gnawed ones, not at all; there's as much meat on them as on the leg of a goose. Then there is a smoked ham throne, and leading up to it, steps of the purest bacon fat. And on those steps there is a carpet entirely made of sausage skins, and on top of the sausage skins is a layer of hash as thick as a finger – "

Fido couldn't stand it any longer. He rushed out into the field and called: "Bow–wow, where is that treasure? Bow--wow, where is the dogs' treasure?"

But at that moment all the fairy dogs and the aged fairy dog suddenly disappeared. Fido rubbed his eyes; there was nothing there but a silver meadow, not a blade of grass had been rumpled by the fairies' dance, not a drop of dew had fallen to the ground. Just a peaceful moon shone on a pleasant field, and the forest stood all round like the blackest of ramparts.

And then Fido remembered that there was at least some bread soaked in water waiting for him at home, and he ran home as fast as his legs would carry him. But ever since then, when he again went with Grandad over the meadows or through the forest, he remembered now and then the dogs' treasure fallen deep into the earth, and he would begin to dig, to dig furiously with all four paws, making a deep hole in the earth. And as he probably must have let the secret out to the dogs in the neighbourhood, and they in turn to others, and the others to yet more, it happens to all the dogs in the world that somewhere in a field they remember the buried dogs' kingdom and they dig in the earth and sniff and smell, whether they can't catch a whiff from the depths of the earth of that smoked ham throne of the former dogs' kingdom.

17

THE FIRST
GANGSTERS' TALE

My Fat Great-Grandfather
and the Gangsters

My deceased great-grandfather was a wheelwright by trade and apart from that he did a bit of horse handling now and then, and traded in clover seed. At the age of ninety-eight he was, praise be, an active and merry old fellow, round and red as an apple; indeed he was so extraordinarily fat, that in summer my great-grandmother stored him in the cellar, because upstairs the heat would have dissolved him. So he settled down nicely in the cellar, sipped his sugared beer and looked forward to cooler weather.

When the hot summer was over he crept out, pottered about minding his own business, he managed, supervised and arranged, bought, sold and hunted for goods, fixed things up, hammered them down and carpentered, he sweated and slogged away, stamping in his bedroom slippers and stumping around in his brogues, ate and drank hugely, in fact at his venerable age and with such estimable girth, he carried on so nicely that everybody was pleased. And he had, I can tell you, the most noble belly in the whole parish, for which the parish was justly proud of him. There was no one else to match him: so fat and red, so broad-chested and waddling, with such wrinkles round his eyes and such a button nose and so many double chins. Even in other parishes there was no such man. When he came to the market in Market Harborough everybody turned round to gaze after him, whether student, bishop or general, hungry student or frowning general dried up like a kipper. Even the bishop himself was not nearly so fat or so ruddy, so bulky, or waddled so beautifully as my deceased great-grandfather.

His face was clean-shaven. His nose, cheeks and ears were red verging on purple; round his neck he would tie a stripy handkerchief, a mighty waistcoat arched over his stomach with two rows of metal buttons, and in it he had an enormous snuff-box that held a pound of snuff all at once. There he would stand, amongst the carters and farmers, the millers and wheelwrights, and he talked and expounded, or he would sit in the pub when his feet ached, and there he talked and expounded and cracked jokes. Ah no! such old-world and thorough-going people don't exist any longer. And then, too, such extraordinary things happened to my great-grandfather, such as don't occur nowadays.

For instance, one day he had sold a horse and was going home with his dog Mutt and several hundred in his pocket, when a great storm surprised him in the hills. As my great-grandfather preferred beer to water, he quickly looked around to find some pub where he could wait nicely in the dry till the downpour and thunder had passed. There was no house far and wide but one wretched inn called "The Hanged Man and Bottle". As the name implies, this inn had no good reputation. But, as there was no other shelter anywhere near, there was nothing my great-grandfather could do but take refuge under that roof, though he did so unwillingly, and only because the downpour was soaking him to the skin and Mutt to the bone, and he cursed the storm as he trotted – so far as his breath permitted – to the pub, where all the windows shone with light.

19

But my good great-grandfather and Mutt could never have imagined even in their dreams that they would arrive in the middle of a gangsters' ball. Yes, the very worst gangsters were just holding a ball there, and all of them had put on some kind of fancy dress. The chief of all the robbers was there, the famous Robber Baron himself, in a tailcoat, white tie and white gloves like a great gentleman; his mistress, the sly and powdered Cocotte, dressed as a ballet dancer, the notorious murderer Cutthroat was disguised in pale blue and pink satin as a page. There was the Black Knave, Bloody Bob and Shyster the con man, and Ratface and the wicked Ripper and the international villain Dynamite and the double-crosser Cadster; in short the whole bunch of them, and they had put on the masks and costumes of Turks, Chinamen, bears and drummers, organ-grinders, knights and jesters, the way it is at fancy-dress balls. There they were, turning about, feasting and chatting like ordinary decent and honest people, but you could see from their spiteful eyes that they were up to no good. And under their wigs their hair bristled up and their faces were scarred. Bloody Bob had two fingers missing from his left hand, but the remaining fingers were full of rings. None of their hands were work-worn, but they had great thieving joints and filthy nails, and some of them had dirty ears too, because they were always thinking up some scoundreldom and then they forgot to wash properly with soap and warm water. They just wipe their faces over with their paws like a cat and think that's good enough. So, boys, remember that and have a good wash when Mummy tells you in the morning.

Well, so great-grandfather was much amazed that he'd come in the middle of a ball, he was a bit afraid, but it didn't occur to him at once that they could be real gangsters. Mutt snorted and shook himself, and I don't think he

thought anything at all. So great-grandfather said: "I wish the company a nice evening!" sat down away in a corner and ordered beer and cheese. And then one of the gangsters, who was feasting on steak and nibbling with it alternately gherkins, ice cream and eclairs, said: "Wish you good appetite!" and Grandad replied politely: "And I wish the same to you," because he set store by good manners. But of course the gangsters, seeing they'd got an honest man on their hands, intended nothing good and wanted to have some nasty fun at his expense.

So they started off. "Mister Roly-poly," twittered Cocotte, as if great-granfather's name wasn't Smith, "you and I would make a fine couple! I'll book you a quadrille, a highland fling, or better still a mazurka." The gangsters hooted with laughter. Cocotte was so terribly thin, and how could great-grandfather do a mazurka? Great-grandfather was cross about that insolent form of address and the laughter. He thought of great-grandmother and, as I say, Cocotte was as thin as a rake. The girl needn't have put on such airs. So great-grandfather said, lifting his vast boot with iron staples and hobnails: "I didn't put on my patent leather shoes for dancing and maybe, Missy, I might step on your little toes and, as I see, you have legs like sticks, in fact like matchsticks, and feet, I might say, like a sparrow."

Cocotte didn't care for that reply very much, and she turned frowning to her Robber Baron, that cruel gangster. The Robber Baron tugged ominously at his scruffy moustache: "Ha, d'you know where you are, you wretched farmyard clod? You've fallen among thieves!" Great-grandfather started to sweat in fear: nothing good was going to come of this. "I am the famous Robber Baron," the chief went on, "and that one there with the lute is the notorious murderer Cutthroat, and this Turk here is the much-feared Ripper,

21

that Chinaman is Bloody Bob, the bear is Dynamite, and that drummer is the double-crosser Cadster, the organ-grinder is Ratface, the jester the Black Knave, and the knight is Shyster the con man, all my blood-smirched gentlemen comrades! And this is our gangsters' anthem," said the Robber Baron, and he began to sing:

> *"Friends and gangsters, gentlemen,*
> *thieves, criminals and con men,*
> *murdering and marauding,*
> *lying, cheating, defrauding,*
> *killing, brawling, always stealing,*
> *picking pockets, double dealing,*
> *crime does pay, and that's our game,*
> *come with us and do the same!"*

Upon which the Black Knave sang:

> *"Chains of gold and jewels, hey!*
> *Brooches, rings with precious stones.*
> *Just you look out, man, I say,*
> *when you're caught they'll break your bones!"*

Chorus:

> *"We wish you luck on your way,*
> *we'll be copped too, come the day!"*

Cutthroat:

> *"A loaded pistol is all right,*
> *and a really sharp-edged knife,*
> *but what good's a knife so bright*
> *when you're begging for your life?"*

Chorus:

"Goodbye, brother, for now, don't fail,
or we'll see each other again in jail!"

Bloody Bob:

"Hell's bells and buckets of blood!
Go ahead, stab, shoot and dare!
But if you don't want your face in the mud,
you'd better take pretty good care!"

Chorus:

"Bye–bye, gangsters and fellows,
see you under the gallows!"

That's what the gangsters sang, and during the chorus they all clinked glasses, while Great–Grandfather was stunned that they could sing such a dreadful song and be so merry about it. He thought quickly what to do, and it occurred to him that he should do a bit of blood–curdling himself: so he rolled his eyes terribly, frowned ferociously, made awe–inspiring faces and attempted to lie. "Well, I know all about that," he said. "That's why I came amongst you here. I'm in disguise too. I dressed up as a fat old wheelwright, but actually I'm the famous criminal, thief and multi–murderer Superassassin who, with these very hands, has stabbed, cut down and assassinated sixty men, thirty women and fifteen children, and robbed all the castles, mansions, homes, buildings and cottages in the whole wide region! And that is my police dog, the vicious Jagtooth," added Great–Grandfather, looking round for Mutt.

23

But the rascally gang only hooted. Of course they did, for Mutt was sitting up and begging, humbly asking the feasting gangsters for a bone. And the Robber Baron mockingly lifted up the purse of money, the snuff-box, even the stripy handkerchief, everything that the agile thief, the Black Knave, had taken from the unsuspecting great-grandfather's pocket during his boasting speech. "Just fancy that now," said the Robber Baron, "yet this is, I believe, your own money, your snuff-bow and noserag that the Black Knave has so neatly snaffled. You'll have to be an apprentice to us, my good fellow, if you want to take from others and keep what is yours."

Great-Grandfather scratched his neck: I shan't get out of this mess so easily, he thought. And the gansters immediately started to roar: "He'll have to be an apprentice to us!"

—As I said: first of all they wanted to make a fool of him and give him something to think about, and who knows what else of the very worst they intended later.

And Shyster the Con Man started off: "Tell us, apprentice, who is it who has what is his in another man's pocket?" Great-Grandfather thought for a bit and said: "That's a man who's been robbed; what was his is in the thief's pocket." "No, all wrong," grinned Shyster, "its the thief. He has his hand in another man's pocket!" Great-Grandfather didn't like that riddle at all: he saw he'd never get anywhere with a swindler like that: if he'd guessed it was the thief they would have jeered at him anyway and said it was the man who'd been robbed, and would never let him guess right.

"And now, Black Knave, tell him what are the qualities that a real thief must have," commanded the Robber Baron.

The Black Knave strutted importantly in front of Great-Grandfather and started his lecture: "A real thief, fleecer or pilferer is black in the night, green in the grass, transparent

in the day: he should be as thin as a wire and as flexible as an eel, so that he can slip through a cup–handle, a keyhole, a chink under the door, a crack in the wall; he must be able to hide under a blade of grass, not breathing or making a sound, he may not sneeze or cough, must know how to climb a wall like a fly, have hands and feet as soft as a cat's, so that doors never creak nor floorboards squeak, so the dog shouldn't bark and wake the owner. He may not have more than a pound of bones in his body and three ounces of flesh, so that he can slip in anywhere, worm his way into any place, hide anywhere, pervade, permeate and penetrate everywhere; if he is heavier or fatter, then he has to be hewn and shaped with an axe, cut and carved with a barking iron, planed and sawn, rubbed, scraped and plucked, smoothed and polished, stretched and bent, softened, stiffened and made pliant, tempered with a flail and cudgel and knocked into shape with a hammer, soaked and made supple and dried, in water, under the earth, in fire and in the air."

My great–grandfathers's hair was standing on end in horror, but already there was Cadster standing in front of him and asking: "And what would you do, apprentice, if you had crept into a house and someone in the next room did wake up after all and called out: "Is there anybody there?" – What would you do?"

"I should be so quiet, I wouldn't utter a sound," answered my great–grandfather.

"Wrong," Ratface laughed at him, "you would answer very loud: "Nobody!" so that the person who'd woken up would be calmed down and would say: "Ah, that's all right then, I just thought there was someone there." – And if he were to shout "Burglars!" you'd answer that it was the water in the pipes gurgling. And if he yelled: "Murder!" you'd assure him

25

you were alive all right, and if again he called "Help!" you would answer politely: "Thanks very much, I can manage to take the lot myself."

"And now," decided Bloody Bob, "we'll teach him how a real thief should set about his robbery. First of all take off your boots, but quick! or we'll know how to hurry you up." he ordered and pointed a pistol at my great-grandfather, one should not jest with gangsters when they want to have a joke. There was nothing Great Grand-father could do but obey, so, puffing and blowing, he started to take off his muddy jackboots. It was extremely hard for him, because of course at home Great-Grandmother always helped him off with his boots, and if Great-Grandmother was not enough, then the other women from the whole place, old mother Stevens and sometimes the Stevens' Mary too, and even Annie and maybe Rosie, and sometimes Stevens himself and Green would help him, and now he was to take off his boots all by himself! But at last the unlucky boots were off, and Great Grandfather appeared, quite out of breath, in the red and green striped stockings Great-Grandmother had knitted him that winter.

"That," said Shyster, "is so that nobody hears you."

Then they took the board on which the inn-keeper chalked up their debts and wrote "Nobody" on it, and hung it on Great-Grandfather's back.

"And that," grinned Dynamite, "is so that nobody sees you."

Then Cutthroat grabbed a handful of soot and blackened Great-Grandfather's face all over and said: "And that is so that nobody recognizes you."

Finally they put into one of his hands a burglar's lamp, hung on twisted string so it spun round ceaselessly, and into the other they shoved burglars' tools, jemmies, special pliers,

axes, saws and chisels, drills, gimlets and picklocks, so –
they said – that he should see well and have everything he
needed at hand.

So that rotten crew made fun of the poor old man, but
the worst was still to come.

"And now you'll show us how you'd creep after the loot
nicely on tip-toe, carefully, so the light from the burglars'
lamp doesn't spin and jump, quietly as a mouse, smoothly
as a snake and lightly as a fly, holding your breath and
stopping at every step, so that not a floorboard creaks, not

a bit of gravel crunches, not a blade of grass rustles, not a murmur is heard! And if the floor does creak or a bit of gravel crunches, a blade rustles or a murmur is heard, we shall hew and shape you with an axe, we shall lighten, cut and slice you with a knife, plane and file you with plane and file, temper and knock you with flail, cudgel and hammer, soften you, stiffen you and make you supple, soak you, squeeze you, dry you, under the earth, in fire and in the air!"

My great-grandfather got shivers up his spine when he heard what a difficult task they had set him. But he was in their power and had to obey. The gangsters had formed a ring round him like at the circus and were looking forward to the show.

"Hola hop!" shouted the Robber Baron.

Great-Grandfather held his breath and tried to creep along on the tips of his toes. But alas! He was too heavy and had that waddling gait, and he couldn't keep his balance. He tried to place his old feet lightly and gently, as if walking on eggs, but at every little step the floor creaked frightfully, his knee-joints cracked aloud and he swayed unsteadily, like on a tightrope, and when he balanced with his hands all those burglars' files, hammers, pliers, chisels, drills and picklocks rattled mightily, and the sweat broke out on his forehead and he panted excessively – and the gangsters guffawed, holding their sides, the devil take them, the miserable wretches, for laughing at age and grey hairs like that!

But hark! Suddenly a great noise could be heard from outside, the beat of horses' hoofs, the clatter of carriages and hooting of cars and rumbling of planes. It gave the gangsters a jolt and they stopped laughing at once. While they had been making fun of my great-grandfather they had completely forgotten to keep watch so that no one surprised them. They had good reason to be afraid, gang

of blackguards that they were. And then all that great racket came to a halt in front of the pub. The gangsters paled. Damn it! It might be a general with his soldiers, or a governor with an armed escort, or the supreme chief of police himself with his constables, guards and beadles, sent to surround the thieving band with superior numbers and arrest them, fetter them and carry them off to the gallows!

The gangsters quaked with fear; it was too late to flee and they all turned helplessly towards their chief. The Robber Baron stood there, tugged at his extra–long moustache and thought. Then he raised the first finger of his right hand, tapped his forehead a couple of times and said: "Ha, I've got it! All of you stand completely still like statues and don't bat an eyelid till I tell you. I'll fix the rest myself!" So the gangsters stood still like statues, and steps were already approaching from the passage; it was high time.

The door opened and in came – not a general with his soldiers, nor a governor, nor even the supreme chief of police, but the high and mighty Lord Havelock of London, who was travelling there with a large entourage of servants and lackeys, cooks, personal doctors and chemists, bodyguards, detectives and policemen.

Of course Lord Havelock was surprised when he saw the motionless figures of a Chinaman, a ballet dancer and a Turk, a bear, a drummer, a jester, a page and an organ–grinder. He stopped in the doorway, put his monocle in his eye, looked round and said: "Ah!" That is an English word and in Czech it is ah! too. Then he went on with English sang–froid: "We were overtaken by a storm on our journey, and I intend to stay here with my entourage till morning. Are you perhaps the inn–keeper?" he asked the Robber Baron, who was bowing assiduously behind the table.

"Your Honour," bowed the crafty Robber Baron, "I am

not the inn–keeper, but I am at your service, the renowned Maestro Puppetello, owner of the world–famous strolling theatre company, the astounding show with mobile puppets. Here they are," the Robber Baron pointed around at his motionless gangsters. "Fifteen years have I worked on them, and perfected them for another five. Each puppet is full of little cog–wheels, hooks and levers, all electric, no tricks. Each one is differently dressed, each one has been taught a different task, they are almost indistinguishable from human beings. The storm caught me here with my little company on our way to the most distinguished royal and ducal courts, from which I have innumerable letters of praise and recognition, orders and decorations."

"Ah!" said the lord, "and what can your mobile puppets do?"

"Your Honour," the Robber Baron bent in a servile bow, "Maestro Puppetello had not intended to give a performance here. But, feeling infinitely honoured by your esteemed interest, I shall allow myself in all humility to present my whole show to you."

Lord Havelock raised his second monocle and sat down in the midst of his entourage. The Robber Baron once more bowed to the ground and announced: "A special performance for his lordship, Lord Havelock!" He straightened his waistcoat and, in his white tie and white gloves, he stepped up to Cocotte first, who stood there motionless in her ballet costume, not batting an eyelid, like a wax figurine in a shop window. The Robber Baron pretended to press a secret button on her back, called "A ballet dancer!" and hey presto! – for that gang of tricksters knew its way about any form of cheating at once – Cocotte shook a thin little leg, raised an arm, gave a sweet smile, did a few dance steps and turned around gracefully several times, and

30

when she had danced back to her place she shook her thin leg again, put down her arm and stood motionless.

"Ah," said the lord, "that's very nice."

So then the Robber Baron stepped up to the Ripper, dressed as a Turk, pretended to press a secret button on his back, winked at him and announced "A Turk!" and behold, first there was a rattling inside the Turk, as though he was a machine, then the Turk jerked once or twice, folded his arms across his chest, bowed three times and pronounced very distinctly the Turkish greeting: "Salaam alaikum."

"Ah," said the lord, "that's very nice too."

Then the Robber Baron set off Bloody Bob, representing a Chinaman. Inside the Chinaman too there was a rattling and a twitching, then he raised his hands with both first fingers stuck up in the air, bowed three times and three times repeated the greeting" "Chee chu ha, chiri miri ho."

"Ah," said the lord, "a fine Chinaman."

In this way the Robber Baron presented the whole of his company to his lordship: Cutthroat with his lute, who tinkled a song, then the knight Shyster knelt down, made a bow and called "hurrah" three times, the jester Black Knave did a somersault, the bear Dynamite growled and turned round clumsily, while the drummer Cadster drummed an accompaniment for him and the organ–grinder Ratface turned the handle of his barrel–organ.

"Ah," said the lord, "beautiful clockwork puppets. How much do you want for them, Maestro Puppetello?"

"Your Honour," answered the Robber Baron, "as it is for you, I'll let you have them cheap. Be so good as to decide on their value yourself."

"I'll give you a hundred thousand," the lord decided. "My treasurer will pay that out to you tomorrow. I shall stand the puppets in my bedroom."

31

That was something for the Robber Baron when he saw how the lord was walking straight into his trap. What a wonderful opportunity for his gang, when everyone was asleep, to murder the lord and get away with vast booty!

"Your Honour," he bowed insidiously, "I am quite delighted that my puppets will receive the great honour of spending some time in your esteemed company."

Lord Havelock, well satisfied, was just getting up from his chair when his eye fell on my great-grandfather standing there in the corner in his striped stockings, with his soot-smeared face and a board on his back. "Ah," said the lord, "and what can this puppet do, Maestro Puppetello?"

But our friend the Robber Baron had forgotten all about my great-grandfather, and now he couldn't quickly think up any role for him. So he got completely confused and began to stammer: "That is – if you please – that is – er – well – Nobody. You see – its not finished yet."

But my great-grandfather wasn't born yesterday, and he thought that now it was his turn to give the gangsters a proper fright. The Robber Baron had not even come to the end of his stammering when my great-grandfather started to play the role the gangsters had themselves taught him a few moments before. Right out of the blue, before their eyes, he began to creep on tip-toe like a thief.

The Robber Baron was struck dumb, the lord in his surprise put on a third monocle, he cried "ah". and the whole of his entourage cried "ah" with him.

At first my great-grandfather crept up to Cadster, reached into his clothes and dragged out of his pockets all his picklocks, drills, chisels and gimlets and other burglars' tools, and as he did so he sang the first verse of the gangsters' anthem:

"Friends and gangsters, gentlemen,
thieves, criminals and con men,
killing, brawling, always stealing,
picking pockets, double dealing,
crime does pay, and that's our game,
come with us and do the same!"

"Ah," said Lord Havelock, and with him his whole entourage. The Lord's first adjutant detective Sherlock Holmes pricked up his ears: he began to feel that something was up.

And now my great-grandfather began to sing the second verse of the gangsters' anthem:

"Chains of gold and jewels, hey!
Brooches and rings with precious stones.
Just look out, Black Knave, I say,
when you're caught they'll break your bones!"

And he went up to the Black Knave and as he sang he pulled out of his pockets the stolen jewels, golden rings, bracelets, watches and necklaces. It almost amounted to a whole jeweller's shop.

"Ah," cried Lord Havelock and with him his entourage. The Lord's second adjutant detective, Stuart Webbs, pricked up his ears: he began to surmise that something was up.

And my great-granfather sang:

"A loaded pistol is all right,
and a really sharp-edged knife,
but Cutthroat, what's a knife so bright
when you're begging for your life?"

33

and from under Cutthroat's clothes he pulled out all his murderous weapons, knives and pistols and daggers.

"Ah," cried Lord Havelock and with him his retinue.

The Lord's third adjutant detective, Joe Deebs, pricked up his ears, and began to feel that something was up.

Thus my great-grandfather went through all the verses of the song with one gangster after another, taking out their criminal tools and stolen goods and murderous weapons and laying them all on the floor. Lord Havelock always cried "ah!" and with him his whole entourage, and successively the lord's adjutant detectives Higgs, Lutz, Leblanc and Pitt, pricked up their ears.

Great-Grandfather left the Robber Baron till the last. Out of his pocket he took his own purse of money, his snuff-box, from which he immediately gave himself a big sniff, and his stripy handkerchief, into which he trumpeted as loudly as a French horn, and at the same time he sang:

> *"Hell's bells and buckets of blood!*
> *Go ahead, stab, shoot and dare!*
> *But if you don't want your face in the mud,*
> *Robber Baron, then take good care!"*

"Ha, the Robber Baron!" called the lord's adjutant detective Clifton, who was by now certain that what was up was the greatly feared Robber Baron and his gang. "The Robber Baron!" called all the lord's adjutant detectives and pulled out their ropes, strait-jackets and handcuffs. "The Robber Baron!" called Lord Havelock, putting his fourth monocle into his eye. "The Robber Baron!" shouted the lord's security guards, constables and beadles, and aimed their guns at the chief and his gang.

"Well, my dear chaps, you'll have to serve your appren-

34

ticeship with me if you want to take from others and keep your own," said my great-grandfather to the gangsters.

They tied up the Robber Baron and the gangsters and took them all away, including Cocotte, and handed them over to justice.

My fat great-grandfather put on his boots and washed his face, and Lord Havelock thanked him for saving him from such terrible danger. He gave him, amongst other things, a beautiful snuff-box, filled with sweet-smelling snuff, from which Great-Grandfather afterwards gave a sniff to all wheelwrights, horse handlers and traders in clover seed from the whole district.

Great Grandfather called Mutt, who had in the meantime been stuffing himself in the corner with the remains of the gangsters' feast, so he could hardly move. Great-Grandmother welcomed them home very peevishly, for once more coming home so late from the pub, but when my great--grandfather related to her all that had happened, she was truly glad that it had all turned out so well.

A GREAT DOCTORIAL TALE

It is indeed a long time ago now that the magician Magus carried out his sorcerer's trade on Haystack Hill. As you know, there are good magicians, who are known as wizards or workers of wonders, and bad magicians, known as necromancers. Magus was somewhere in between; sometimes he was so good that he didn't make magic at all, and other times he made such mighty magic that it caused thunder and lightning; sometimes it occurred to him to make it rain stones, and once he even made it rain little frogs. Briefly, say what you like, a magician like that is by no means a pleasant neighbour, and even though people swore they did not believe in magicians, they preferred to avoid Haystack Hill. They were only making excuses when they said the hill was too steep to climb – of course they weren't going to admit they were afraid of Magus!

Well, one day this Magus was sitting in front of his lair eating plums – those big blue–black bullaces with a beautiful sheen on them – while inside the cave his apprentice, freckle–faced Vincie, full name Vincent Nickelkins of Zickleton, was stirring over the fire magical concoctions that were made of pitch, sulphur, valerian, mandrake, devil's–bit, gall nuts, deadnettle, scorzonera, also of cart–grease and hell–pebbles,

of trendymendy and aqua regia and goat's dung, of wasp stings, rat's whiskers, moth's legs and Zanzibar seed, that is of all kinds of magical spices, charlatan's potions and wormwood. And Magus just watched freckle–faced Vincie stirring and went on eating plums. But poor little Vincie somehow forgot to stir or whatever, and briefly those concoctions in the cauldron somehow got a bit singed, slightly burnt, somewhat scorched, sizzled, smouldered or scalded, and gave off a terrible stench.

"You ham–fisted clumsy fool," Magus wanted to shout at him, but in his hurry he must have mistaken the right pipe in his throat, or the plum he had in his mouth mistook it, in short he swallowed the plum with the stone, and that stone went down the wrong way and got stuck in his throat, and it could go neither up nor down; and so Magus only had time to shout: "You ham–" and couldn't go on, he couldn't even let out a squeak. He just wheezed and croaked, like steam hissing out of a kettle, and got red in the face and waved his hands and choked, but the stone wouldn't budge a mite, so firmly and thoroughly was it wedged in his throat.

When Vincie saw this he got terribly scared that maybe Old Man Magus would suffocate, and he said ever so helpfully: "You just wait here, Boss, I'll hop over to Grimstone for a doctor." And off he shot down Haystack Hill – its a pity there was no one there to time him – it would certainly have been a world record for the marathon.

When he got to Grimstone to the doctor's he couldn't even catch his breath, but then he did catch it after all by the right end of the stick and quickly gushed out the words: "Please, Doctor, you must come at once, absolutely at once and double quick to Master Magician Magus, 'cos he's suffocating. My, my! I didn't half run!"

"Magus on Haystack Hill?" growled the Grimstone doctor.

37

"'Pon my word! I'm not really keen on that, but if he needs me at all costs then it can't be helped." And he went. You see, a doctor can't refuse to help anybody, even if they called him to Robber Reprobatius or even (God have mercy on us!) to Lucifer himself. That's the sort of profession it is, that doctoring.

So the Grimstone doctor took his doctor's bag, that had in it doctor's scalpels and forceps for teeth and bandages and pills and ointments and splints for broken bones and other such doctor's tools, and he went after Vincie to Haystack Hill. "I hope we are not too late," freckle–faced Vincie kept on worrying, and so they went, right, left, right, left, o–ver hills and rills, right, left, right, left, across bogs, right, left, right, left, through thick and thin, till freckle–faced Vincie said: "Well, Doctor, here we are."

"At your service, Mr. Magus," said the Grimstone doctor, "what seems to be the trouble?"

Instead of answering Magus the magician just croaked, wheezed and panted and puffed and pointed to his throat, to show that that was where the trouble was.

"Ah, a sore throat," said the Grimstone doctor. "Well, we'll take a look at that little hurtie place. Open your mouth nice and wide, Mr. Magus, and say aah."

Magician Magus parted his black beard and opened his mouth wide, but he couldn't say aah, because he couldn't get a sound out.

"Come on now, aah!" the doctor encouraged him. "Can't you manage that?"

Magus shook his head, like he couldn't.

"Oh, dear me," said the doctor, who was a sly fox, a shrewd shyster, an artful bird, a wily wretch and a regular rascal, for he had what it takes and was up to the tricks of the trade, "dear me, Mr. Magus, you really are in a bad way

if you can't say aah. I don't know, I'm sure," he said, and he began to examine Magus and tap him all over, he took his pulse, had a look at his tongue, peered under his eyelid, held up a mirror and shone a light into his ears and up his nose, all the time muttering Latin words to himself. And when he had finished the examination, he started to look extremely grave and said: "Mr. Magus, this is a serious matter, there is nothing for it in this case but the most speedy and immediate operation. But that I cannot and may not do alone, I should have to have some assistance. If you want to undergo an operation, I'm afraid, it can't be helped, you'll have to send for my fellow-doctors in Piddlehinton, White Lackington and Nether Cerne, and when they come I shall hold a medical consultation or concilium with them and only after the gravest consideration should we then undertake the requisite medical intervention or operation operandi. Think it over, Mr. Magus, and if you accept my suggestion, send a speedy messenger for my highly esteemed and learned doctoral colleagues."

What could Magus do? He nodded to freckle-faced Vincie and Vincie stamped three times, so as to get off to a good start, and there he was rushing down Haystack Hill. To Piddlehinton. And to White Lackington. And to Nether Cerne. For the moment let us leave him running.

About the Soliman Princess

While freckle–faced Vincie was racing along to Piddlehinton and to White Lackington and to Nether Cerne for doctors, the Grimstone doctor sat by Magus and saw to it that he didn't suffocate entirely. So as to pass the time more quickly, he lit up a cigar and smoked in silence.

When the time seemed to go very slowly, he cleared his throat and went on smoking. Then, as a pastime, he yawned three times and blinked. After some time he sighed: "Ah, well!" Then half an hour later he stretched his back and said: "There now!" After an hour or so he added: "Perhaps in the meantime we could play cards. Have you any cards here, Mr. Magus?"

Magus the magician couldn't speak, so he just shook his head, to show he hadn't.

"No cards?" growled the Grimstone doctor. "That's a pity. A fine magician you must be if you haven't even any cards! We had a magician perform in our pub, just a moment, what was his name now? Something like Evans or Don Bosko or Magorello, something like that, and I can tell you he did such magical tricks with cards as would amaze you. Well of course, one has to know how to make magic."

41

Then he lit up another cigar and said: "Well then, if you haven't any cards, I'll tell you the tale of the Soliman princess, to hurry time along a bit. If you should happen to know this fairy–tale, just tell me and I'll stop at once. Ting–a–ling, here we go.

As everyone knows, beyond the Jackdaw Mountains and the Sargasso Sea there are the Dalliance Islands, and beyond them is the Sharivari Desert, covered in thick forest, with the main gypsy capital Eldorado; then spread far and wide there is one meridian of longitude and one parallel of latitude and there, just beyond the river, where you go across the little footbridge and then take the path to the left, passing the willow bush and the burdock ditch, lies the great and mighty Soliman sultanate. So now you know exactly, don't you?

In the Soliman sultanate, as the name implies, Sultan Soliman reigned. That sultan had one daughter, Zubayda her name was, and – just out of the blue – that Princess Zubayda started to be ill and feel sick, she coughed and languished and pined and grew thin and pale, she grieved and sighed, it was misery to see her. Of course the sultan hastily summoned to her bed his court magicians, exorcists, wizards, witches, sibyls, seers and astrologers, charlatans and quacks, spa–keepers and sawbones and vets, but none of them could cure the princess. If it had been here in our country, I would have said that the girl was suffering from anaemia, pleurisy and bronchial catarrh, but in Soliman's land there is not such a high standard of education and medicine is not as far advanced as to have illnesses with Latin names. You can imagine how desperate the old sultan was. Oh Monte Christo! he said to himself. I was so much looking forward to my girl's taking over a flourishing sultan's business from me, and instead the poor child is

wasting and fading away before my eyes, and I cannot even help her! – And so a great sadness reigned at the court and in the whole of Soliman's country.

At that time there came a commercial traveller from Jablonec, a certain Mr. Lustig, and when he heard of the sick princess he said: "My lord the sultan should summon a doctor from our place, meaning Europe, because there medicine is more advanced; here you only have exorcists, herbalists and shamans, but we have, I tell you, real educated doctors."

When Sultan Soliman heard about it, he called for that Mr. Lustig, bought a string of glass pearls from him for Princess Zubayda, and then asked him: "Mr. Lustig, how can you tell, in your country, whether a man is a real, educated doctor?"

"Oh, that's quite easy," said Mr. Lustig. "You can tell according to whether he has Dr in front of his name. For instance, Dr Man, Dr Pellner and suchlike. And if he has no Dr, then he's not a qualified doctor, you see?" "Ah, I see," said the sultan, and he richly rewarded Mr. Lustig with sultanas – those nice raisins, you know. And then he sent messengers to Europe for a doctor. "But remember," he instructed them when saying goodbye, "that a real qualified doctor is only one whose name begins with the syllable Dr. Don't you bring me anyone else, or I'll cut off your ears and your heads along with them. So get moving!"

If I were to tell you all the things those envoys underwent and experienced on the long, long way to Europe, Mr. Magus, that would make a long story indeed. But after many, many hardships those messengers did, after all, reach Europe, and they began to search for a doctor for Princess Zubayda.

So the procession of Soliman's messengers, hulking

43

great oafs with turbans on their heads and fuzz under their noses as thick and long as a horse's tail, set off on the path through a dark forest. They walked and they walked, till they met a fellow with an axe and a saw on his shoulder.

"Top of the morning to you," the fellow greeted them.

"And to you," the messengers said. "And what do you do, my good man?"

"Well," said the man, "thanks for your interest. Actually I'm a drover, but just now I'm a hewer of wood and a drawer of water."

Those heathens pricked up their ears at that, and they said: "That's another matter, Your Excellency. If we have the honour of speaking to Dr Over, then we are to ask you to go hotfoot and skedaddle like greased lightning with us to the land of Soliman. Sultan Soliman sends his best respects and invites you most deferentially to his court; but should you hesitate or be reluctant in any way, then we'll drag you there by force, and I can assure you, revered Sir, that that is hardly something you would enjoy!"

"Well, really," the drover, now woodcutter, was surprised, "and what does the sultan want me to do?"

"He's got a job of work for you," said the messengers.

"Then I wouldn't mind going," the woodcutter agreed. "You see the fact is, gentlemen, I am just now looking for work. I'm a real dragon for work."

The messengers winked at each other and said: "Now that, Your Worship, is just what we need."

"Just a moment," said the woodman. "First of all I want to know how much this sultan of yours is going to pay me for my work. I'm not an idle drone just craving for money, but I hope the sultan doesn't dry up on payments."

Sultan Soliman's messengers replied politely: "It doesn't matter, Your Lordship, that you are not Dr One, we are

44

equally happy that you are Dr Over, but as concerns our
Sultan Soliman, you can believe us that he is no Dr Yupon,
but just an ordinary ruler and tyrant."

"That's all right then," said the drover or woodman. "And
as for food, when I'm at work I eat like a drain and drink like
a dromedary, you get me?"

"We shall do all in our power, Esteemed Sir," those

Soliman's men assured him, "to see that you should be entirely satisfied in that respect in our country."

Whereupon, they accompanied the woodman with great pomp and circumstance to the ship and they sailed with him to Soliman's land. When they arrived Sultan Soliman quickly climbed up onto the throne and ordered them to be brought to him. The messengers knelt down before him, and the oldest and most thickly moustached of them began:

"Oh, most merciful lord and sovereign, prince of all believers, my lord Sultan Soliman! At your revered command we betook ourselves as far as that island named Europe, in order to search for the most learned, most highly reputed, most famous doctor for Princess Zubayda. Well, here he is, great sultan. This is the most excellent and world–famous doctor, Dr Over; and so that you should know what kind of a doctor he is, he works like Dr Agon, is paid like Dr One, he eats like Dr Ain and drinks like Dr Omedary. For those, Esteemed Sultan, are all famous and educated doctors, from which it is evident that we caught the right man. And – er – that's about all."

"I welcome you, Dr Over," said Sultan Soliman. "And I would ask you to go and have a look at my daughter, Princess Zubayda."

Well, why shouldn't I? the drover said to himself; and the sultan led him in person to such a dusky, shady chamber, lined with the most beautiful carpets and pillows and cushions, and on them rested Princess Zubayda, pale as wax, slumbering.

"Oh dear," said the drover–cum–woodman sympathetically, "Sir Sultan, that girl of yours is a bit greenery––yallery."

46

"That she is," sighed the sultan.

"A bit wan," said the woodman. "Washed out, you might say, isn't she?"

"Just so," nodded the sultan sadly. "She won't eat a bite."

"Thin as a rake," said the woodman. "Just a wisp, she is. A scrap off colour, Sir Sultan. I'd say the lassie is ailing."

"Of course she's ailing," said the sultan despondently. "That's why I summoned you, so you could cure her, if you're Dr Over."

"What, me?" the woodman was astonished. "Lands'-sakes! How am I to cure her?"

"That's your business," said Sultan Soliman in a dark voice. "That's what you're here for, no two ways about it. But I can tell you, if you don't heal her I'll have your head chopped off and that'll be the end of you."

"But you can't do that," the frightened woodman wanted to protest, but Soliman didn't let him get a word in edge-ways.

"No excuses," he said sternly. "I've no time for anything like that. I have to go and rule. Just you get on with your job and show us what you can do." And he went and sat on the throne and ruled.

"Now here's a pretty kettle of fish!" the woodman said to himself when he was alone, "this is a fine mess I've got into! How on earth am I to fix it so I cure some princess or other? Do I know how its done? I'm in a proper pickle! For five blows to a tree–trunk! What am I to do? If I don't cure the girl, they'll cut my head off. If it wasn't in a fairy–tale I'd say you can't just chop someone's chump off for no-thing, no reason at all. The devil of it is that I've got into a fairy–story. In ordinary life something like that could never happen to me. For crying out loud, I wonder how I'm going to wriggle out of this one!

With such, and even weightier thoughts, the poor woodman

47

sat on the threshold of the sultan's castle and sighed. In the name of goodness, he said to himself, where on earth did they get the idea that I should act as a doctor here? If they'd told me to cut down this tree or that tree, then I'd have shown them what I could do! I'd have spat on my hands and got down to it till the splinters flew. And, as I look at it, I see the whole place is overgrown like a jungle, the sun can't even get through to the sitting-room, why the entire house must be full of damp and fungi and mould and earwigs! Just let them wait, I'll show them how I can polish off a job!

No sooner had he said it than he threw off his coat, spat on his hands, grabbed his axe and saw and set to to cut down those trees growing round the sultan's palace. And those trees, you must know, were no apples and pears, nor nut-trees like in our country, they were all palms and oleanders and cocoanut trees, dragon trees, lataniers and figs and mahogany trees and trees that reach up to heaven and other exotic greenery. And you should have seen, Mr. Magus, how that woodcutter of ours let fly at them! When the noon bell rang there was already quite a clearing round the castle; and then the woodman wiped the sweat off his brow with his sleeve, took from his pocket a bit of black bread with cottage cheese that he had brought from home, and stuck his teeth into his lunch.

Till then Princess Zubayda had been asleep in her dusky bower; through all the racket the woodcutter had been making down below the castle with his axe and his saw, she slept as she had never slept before. What woke her up was the silence, when the woodcutter stopped felling trees, made himself comfortable on a pile of wood and bit into his bread and cheese.

Then the princess opened her eyes and was amazed:

what was all that unusual light in the room? For the first time in her life the sun came streaming into the room and filled that twilight chamber with the light of heaven. The princess was quite dazzled by the flood of light: and through the window came the scent of fresh-cut wood, so strong and beautiful, that the princess breathed in deeply and delightedly. And into that smell of resin there came another smell that the princess did not know – what was it? She got up and went to look out of the window: instead of damp shade a clearing was bright in the noonday sun, and there was a large fellow sitting there, and eating with the greatest appetite something black and something white; and that was the thing that smelt so good to the princess. You know how it is, someone else's lunch always smells the best.

The princess couldn't resist it; that smell drew her down, out in front of the castle, nearer and nearer to that lunching fellow, so that she could have a look at what the good thing was that he was gobbling up.

"Ah, Princess," the woodman greeted her with his mouth full. "Wouldn't you like a bite of bread and cheese?"

The princess blushed and shifted from one foot to the other; she was ashamed to say she was longing terribly to taste it.

"There you are then," mumbled the woodman, and he cut off a great chunk with his jack-knife. "There, you get outside of that."

The princess glanced around, to see whether there wasn't anybody looking. "Ta," she blurted out in thanks, and bit into the slice of bread, then she said:

"Yum, that IS good!" I ask you, bread and cottage cheese, no princess had ever seen anything like that.

At that moment Sultan Soliman himself looked out of the window. He couldn't believe his eyes: instead of the damp

49

shade a bright clearing was gleaming in the noonday sun, and there on a pile of wood sat the princess with her sweet little mouthie full, a moustache of cottage cheese from ear to ear, tucking in with such an appetite as she had never shown.

"Thanks be," Sultan Soliman breathed out, "so they really did bring me the right learned doctor for my little girl."

And ever since then, Mr. Magus, the princess did in fact grow stronger, her cheeks became rosy and she ate like a wolf-cub. That's the effect of light and air and sunshine, you should know. And I'm telling you about it because you too live here in a cave where the sun never shines and the wind never blows: and that, Mr. Magus, is not healthy. That is what I wanted to tell you."

When the Grimstone doctor had finished telling his tale about the Soliman princess, freckled Vincie came running up, and he brought with him the doctor from Piddlehinton, the doctor from White Lackington, and the doctor from Nether Cerne. "Well, I've brought them," he shouted from a distance. "And I can tell you, I'm right out of breath!"

"I welcome you, fellow-doctors," said the Grimstone doctor. "Here is our patient, Mr. Magician Magus. As you observe at first glance, his condition is very serious. The patient indicates that he swallowed a plum or prune, damson, bullace or plumstone. In my humble opinion he is suffering from acute plumbitis."

"Hm, ha," said the doctor from Piddlehinton, "I should rather judge his illness to be strangulating prunivitis."

"I should not like to differ in any way from my respected colleagues," said the Nether Cerne doctor, "but I judge that we have here a case of stonealgia."

"Gentlemen," the White Lackington doctor spoke up, "I propose that we come to common consent on the diagnosis

that in the case of Mr. Magus there is an occurrence of severe plumbolaryngostonealgic prunivitis."

"Well, I must congratulate you, Mr. Magus," said the doctor from Piddlehinton. "That is a very rare and grave disease."

"Indeed, an interesting case," added the doctor from White Lackington.

"But, my dear colleague," piped up the Nether Cerne doctor, "I have in the past had nicer and more interesting medical cases. Did you ever hear about how I cured the Howler of Roarington? If not, I shall be glad to tell you."

The Case of the Howler

"It is a good few years now since this Howler lived in the forest in Roarington. He is, you know, one of the most objectionable bogies there ever was. You are walking through a wood at night and suddenly behind you there is this howling, groaning, wailing, bawling, caterwauling, or the most frightful laughter. Naturally you are scared out of your wits, such terror seizes you that you run, rush, race along, so its a wonder you don't give up the ghost for fear.

Well, all that was done by Howler, that was the mischief he did in Roarington for years and years, so that people were afraid to go there after dark.

And then one day there came into my consulting room such a strange little man, all mouth he was, his kisser stretched from ear to ear, his throat was tied up in a rag, and he wheezed, croaked hoarsely, hawked, screeched and spluttered, till you couldn't understand a word he said.

"Well, what seems to be the trouble?" I said.

"Doctor," grated this fellow, "if you please, I'm a bit hoarse."

"I can see that," I replied, "and who are you?"

The patient squirmed a bit and then burst out: "If you please, Sir, I'm the Howler from Roarington Hill."

"Aha," I said, "so you're that rascal, that wicked creature

52

that haunts people in the forest? Then I can tell you, it just serves you right that you've lost your voice! Do you suppose I'm going to cure your laryngopharyngitis or thratarrh of the coat, I mean to say catarrh of the throat, so that you can go on screeching in the woods and giving people the spasms? No, no, you just go on your way croaking and creaking, at least we'll be rid of you!"

And then this Howler started to plead: "I beg you, for God's sake Doctor, cure me of this hoarseness, I 'll be good, I won't frighten people–"

"I should advise you not to," I said. What with all that scaring people you've over–shouted yourself, that's why you've lost your voice, you see? I can tell you, my boy, haunting a forest is no job for you: the forest is chilly and damp and you have rather delicate respiratory organs. I don't know I'm sure, if it is possible that your catarrh could be cured, but you'd have to leave off haunting and move far, far away from any forest. Otherwise there's not a soul alive that could cure you."

That Howler grew very gloomy and scratched his ear: "That's a very difficult matter, Sir, how shall I earn a living if I give up haunting? I don't know how to do anything but howling and roaring, that is when my voice is all right."

"But, my good fellow," I said to him, "with such rare vocal chords as yours I would join the opera as a singer, or become a costermonger in the market, a town–crier or maybe a barker in a circus; why, with such a splendid, powerful voice as yours its a pity to live in the country, don't you think? You'd have a better chance in a town."

"I ve sometimes thought that myself," that Howler admitted. "Well, I'll try and make a go of it somewhere else, just as soon as I get my voice back."

And so, gentlemen, I sprayed his throat with iodine, prescribed him chloramphenicol and potassium permanganate for gargling, told him to take "Anginol" and put compresses on his throat. And since that day the Howler has not been heard in Roarington; he really did move away and stopped haunting. Years and years later I heard of him again, and that was from the great town of Hurdy–Burdy. It was said that a certain Howler had gone into politics, and

spoke at meetings with such a loud voice and with such success that he became a member of parliament and he's doing very well to this day.

And I'm telling the whole story here so that Mr. Magus can see that, in the case of some complaints, a change of air can work miracles."

The Case of the Bingham's Melcombe Water Gnome

"I too had an interesting medical experience," the White Lackington doctor took the floor. "Down our way, an old water gnome used to live in the river, below the Bingham's Melcombe bridge, in a web of ash tree and willow roots. Joudal his name was, and a grumpy old chap he was, crotchety, huffy and cantankerous; sometimes he caused floods and now and then he drowned children when they were bathing; in short, people didn't like having him around in that river.

One autumn day the old man turned up in my consulting room, in a green tailcoat with a red kerchief on his neck, and he was puffing and panting, coughing, sneezing, blowing, sniffing, and he mumbled: "Dochtor, I've caught some sort of a chill or other ill, it stabs me here and jabs me there, my back aches, my joints creak, I cough till I'm almost sick, I've a cold like a running river; so I'd like to ask you to write me a prescription."

So I examined him and I told him: "Grandad, what you've got is rheumatism, I can give you this ointment, linament it is, so you know, but that's not all. You must always stay in a warm, dry place, understand?"

"I understand all right," growled the old gaffer, "but as to

that dry and warm place, young Sir, that's hardly possible."

"Why's that?" I ask him.

"You see," says he, "I'm the Bingham's Melcombe water gnome. How am I going to find a warm, dry place in the water? I even have to wipe my nose with the surface of the water, I sleep on water, cover myself with water; only now, as I'm growing old, I've put some soft water in the bed instead of hard, so I can lie more softly. But as to that dry and warm, that's going to be difficult, isn't it?"

57

"Can't be helped, Grandad," I say, "in that cold water your rheumatism's only going to get worse. Old bones, you know, need warmth. And by the way, how old are you, Mr. Waterman?"

"Oh dear me," the old man burbled, "I can't tell you, Doctor, I've been here since heathen times – that'll be some thousand years or so – maybe more. Quite a number of years!"

"There you are," I told him, "at that age you should sit by the stove. Just a moment, I have an idea! Did you ever hear of hot springs?"

"Well, I have heard of them, that I have," muttered the old fellow. "But there aren't any of those here."

"Not here," I agreed, "but there are some in Teplice and in Slovakia, in America and New Zealand and all sorts of other places, only deep underground. And those hot springs, you should know, were created just for rheumaticky old water gnomes. You will simply settle down in one such hot geyser as a hot water gnome, and at the same time, cure your rheumatism."

"Hm, hm," the old man hesitated, "and what actually are the duties of such a hot water gnome?"

"Nothing much," I tell him, "he just has to draw the hot water up from the centre of the earth all the time, so it doesn't get cold. And he let's the excess of that warm water run over the surface of the earth. That's all."

"That ought to be all right." mumbled the Bingham's Melcombe water gnome. "Well then, I'll have a look around for some such hot springs. Thank you very much I'm sure, Dochtor." And he shuffled out of the consulting room – leaving a puddle on the floor.

And you see, my dear colleague, the Bingham's Melcombe water gnome had the sense to obey; he settled down

in Slovakia in a hot spring and he draws so much bubbling water from the depths of the earth that there is an eternally warm spring in that place. And people bathe in that warm spring and it does their rheumatism good too, they come there from all over the world to cure themselves. So you learn a lesson from that, Mr. Magus, and do everything that we doctors advise you to do."

The Case of the Fairies

"I, too, had one very special case," the doctor from Piddlehinton joined in. "One night I was sleeping the sleep of the just, when someone taps on my window and calls: "Doctor, doctor!"

I opened the window and said: "What's the matter? Does anyone need me?"

"Yes," a sweet, anxious voice came out of the darkness. "Come. Come and give us your help."

"Who is there?" I asked. "Who is it calling me?"

"It is I, the voice of the night," came from the shadows. "The voice of the moonlit night. Come."

"Coming!" I said in a dream as I got dressed hurriedly. When I came out in front of the house there was no one there.

Believe me, Sirs, I was pretty nervous. "Hallo!" I called almost in a whisper, "is anyone there? Where am I to go?"

"Follow me, follow me," sobbed a delicate and invisible voice: and I went in the direction from which the voice called, path or no path, across dewy fields and a black forest, the moon was shining and the whole world was numb in frozen beauty. I can assure you gentlemen that I know our neck of the woods inside out, but that moonlight night seemed as unreal as a dream. It does sometimes happen that one finds another world in that part of the country that is dearest to one.

When I had been following that voice for a long time I said to myself, "'pon my soul, if this isn't the Piddle valley."

"Here, doctor, here," the voice called me – it sounded as if a wave on the river had sparkled and splashed, and there I am standing on the banks of the river Piddle in a silver field in the moonshine. In the middle of that field there was something light: maybe a body, maybe just mist, perhaps I heard soft crying, perhaps only the lapping of the water.

"There, there," I said soothingly, "who are we, and where does it hurt us?"

"Oh, doctor," came a trembling little voice from that light on the ground, "I am only a fairy, a wood nymph. My sisters were dancing and I was dancing with them, and then, I don't know, perhaps I tripped over a moon beam, or I slipped on the sparkle that shivers in a dewdrop, I don't know what happened to me; suddenly I was lying down, and I cannot get up, and my poor leg hurts, and hurts, and hurts –"

"Well, Missy," I said, "that will probably be a fracture, that is a broken bone. That can be put right. So you are one of those fairies that dance in the valley here? Just fancy that! And when some young man from Dewlish or Athelhampton gets caught amongst you, you dance him to death's door, don't you? Hum, ha! Do you know, little girl, that that's very naughty? But this time your frolicking turned out badly, eh? That's what comes of your dances!"

"Ach, doctor," moaned that scrap of light in the meadow, "if only you knew how my leg hurts!"

"Of course it hurts," I said, "a fracture has to hurt." And I knelt down beside that fairy, so as to treat her broken leg.

Well, Sirs, I have mended hundreds and hundreds of

broken limbs in my time, but with fairies its the very devil. Their bodies are made of mere rays of light, and their bones of what are known as hard rays – there's nothing you can get hold of, they're rarefied as the breeze, light as mist, and now you try and straighten them, push them into shape, bandage them! I can assure you it was a hell of a niggling job. I tried to bind her up with a cobweb, but the fairy whined: "Ow, that cuts me like ropes!" I wanted to fix that broken leg firmly with a petal of apple blossom, but she burst into tears, "Ah, ah, that weighs on me like a stone."

What was I to do? In the end I stripped off just the shine, the metallic gleam, from the wings of a dragonfly or Odonata, and made two splints of it; I dissolved a moonbeam in a drop of dew into the seven colours of the rainbow, and with the thinnest blue ray I tied those splints to the fairy's broken leg. It was such hard work that I was covered in sweat – it seemed to me that that full moon blazed down like the August sun; and when I was ready I sat down beside that fairy and I said:

"Now, Missy, keep to your bed, you may not move that little leg of yours till the bones knit. But listen to me, my dear, I'm surprised that you and your respected sisters are still here. Why, all the fairies and wood nymphs that always used to be here have long, long ago found a better place –"

"Where?" the fairy breathed out.

"Why, in America. In Hollywood," I said. "The place where they make the films, you know? They act and dance for the films, and for that get money like chaff, and the whole world sees them. That's fame, I can tell you, Missy. All fairies and wood nymphs have long ago gone into films, and all imps and pixies too. If only you could see the dresses and the jewels those fairies have – they would never dream of putting on such a simple little gown as you have on."

"Now then," protested the fairy, "this dress is woven from the glow of fireflies!"

"Exactly," I said. "Nobody wears that any more, and the style is entirely different nowadays."

"With a train?" asked the fairy eagerly.

"That I can't tell you," I said, "I don't understand those matters. You should at least go and have a look at that Hollywood. You can get there via Southampton or Liverpool. But its time I was getting along. It'll be dawn in a while; as far as I know, you fairies are only allowed to appear at night, isn't that so? So goodbye, Missy, and think it over about those films."

I never saw that fairy again, probably the fracture of the tibia healed well. And, would you believe it, since then fairies and wood nymphs have ceased to occur in the Piddle valley. Seems to me what happened was, they went away to Hollywood and went into films. Take a close look when next you go to the cinema: it looks as if there were young ladies and gentlemen moving about on the screen, but they have no bodies, you can't put your hand out and touch them, they're just made of rays; from that you can tell they're nothing but fairies. That's why in the cinema they have to turn out the lights, because the fairies and ghosts and all the rest of those creatures are afraid of the light and only come alive in the dark.

And from that too you can see that no ghosts or other fairy-tale phenomena fit into today's world, unless they find some other more sensible occupation. They have plenty of opportunities for it.

But my goodness, children, what with all this story-telling we almost forgot about the magician Magus! Of course he couldn't chatter or mutter, because right up till now the plum was still stuck in his throat; all he could do was sweat

with fear, roll his eyes and wonder when at last those four doctors were going to help him.

"Well, Mr. Magus," said the doctor from Nether Cerne at last, we shall now proceed with the operation. "But first we shall have to wash our hands, because in surgery the main thing is cleanliness!"

And the four doctors started to wash their hands; first in warm water, then in pure spirit, then in petrol, then in carbolic; then they put on clean white coats – mercy on us, children, now there's going to be an operation! If there's anyone who can't bear to look at it, they'd better shut their eyes!

"Vincie," said the doctor from Piddlehinton, "hold the patient's hands tight, so that he cannot move at all."

"Are you ready, Mr. Magus?" gravely asked the doctor from White Lackington.

Magus just nodded, but as he did so his spirit was so tiny with fear that it would have fitted onto the nail of one finger.

"Now!" called the Grimstone doctor.

At that moment the doctor from Nether Cerne raised his arm and gave the magician Magus such a blow on the back, such a wham on the nape of the neck –

– that it boomed like thunder, and people as far away as Frampton, Winterbourne Abbas, even Long Bredy, looked over their shoulders to see if there wasn't a storm coming;

– that the earth shuddered so that in Tincleton one of the galleries in a deserted mine fell in and in Frampton the church tower quivered;

– that in the whole district right up to Yeovil and Sherborne, and possibly even further, all the pigeons took fright, all the dogs crept into their kennels and all the cats sprang up from the hearth;

65

– and that plum flew out of Magus's throat with such terrible force and speed that it flew beyond Dorchester and only in Woddon did it fall to the ground, where it killed a couple of oxen in the field and burrowed three cubits, two furlongs, one and a half fathoms, seven reeds, four rods, poles or perches and a quarter of a digit into the earth.

So first the plum flew out of Magus's throat and right after it flew the words: "–fisted clumsy fool!" For that was the half that had got stuck in Magus's throat when he had wanted to call freckle-faced Vincie a ham-fisted clumsy fool. But those words did not fly so far, they fell to the ground right beyond Charminster and in doing so they broke an old pear-tree in two.

After that Magus straightened his whiskers and said: "Much obliged, I'm sure."

"A pleasure," answered the four doctors. "The operation was successful."

"But," the White Lackington doctor added immediately, "you should convalesce from that illness for another few hundred years in order to be completely healed, Mr. Magus. I would urgently recommend a change of air and climate, the same as in the case of the Bingham's Melcombe water gnome."

"I agree with my colleague," proclaimed the Grimstone doctor. "You need a lot of sun and air for your health, the same as the Soliman princess. For that reason I should warmly recommend to you a stay in the Sahara desert."

"As for me," chimed in the Nether Cerne doctor, "I am of the same opinion. The Sahara desert will be exceptionally healthy for you, Mr. Magus, for the very reason that no plums grow there that could severely endanger your health."

"I would add my voice to those of my right honourable colleagues," concluded the doctor from White Lackington.

"And as you are a magician, Mr. Magus, you can at least do some research in the desert, and think up how to charm some moisture and crops there, so its a place where people can live and work. That would make a beautiful fairy–tale."

What could the magician Magus do? He thanked all four doctors nicely, packed up his box of tricks and moved away from Haystack Hill to the Sahara desert. Since that time there have been no magicians or wizards in our country, and that is a good thing; but the magician Magus is still alive and he is thinking about how to make magic in the desert so that there are fields and forests and towns and villages there – perhaps you, children, will live to see it.

CONTENTS

KAREL ČAPEK - JOSEF ČAPEK
A DOGGY TALE AND TWO TALES ON TOP

From the Czech original by Karel Čapek: Devatero pohádek a ještě jedna od Josefa Čapka jako přívažek. First published in 1932. A Doggy Tale and A Great Doctorial Tale written by Karel Čapek, The First Gangsters' Tale written by Josef Čapek. Illustrated by Josef Čapek. First edition of this translation. Published by Albatros, Publishing House for Children and Young People, Co. Inc., Prague. Printed in 1997, Czech Republic

ISBN 80–00–00543–3
14/45
13–727–97